Dear Griffyn,
Dream Big!
M. _____

Benjamin Birdie's First Flight

Written By
Michael Dotsikas

Illustrated By
Morgan Spicer

KIDS

BROWN BOOKS KIDS

Benjamin Birdie's First Flight

Brown Books Kids
16250 Knoll Trail Drive, Suite 205
Dallas, Texas 75248
www.BrownBooksKids.com
(972) 381-0009

A New Era in Publishing®

ISBN 978-1-61254-960-6
LCCN 2017930923

Printed in the United States
10 9 8 7 6 5 4 3 2 1

Publisher's Cataloging-In-Publication Data

Names: Dotsikas, Michael. | Spicer, Morgan, illustrator.
Title: Benjamin Birdie's first flight / written by Michael Dotsikas; illustrated by Morgan Spicer.
Description: Dallas, Texas : Brown Books Kids, [2017] | Interest age level: 004-008. | Summary: "A little bird with a BIG dream --anxious to fly and be free. Against his Mama's warnings that he's "not yet ready to fly," Benjamin takes a leap of faith and suddenly finds himself free-falling. Spread your wings and embark with Benjamin Birdie on an extraordinary journey of discovery, determination and teamwork as he strives to get back to his nest."--Provided by publisher.
Identifiers: LCCN 2017930923 | ISBN 978-1-61254-960-6
Subjects: LCSH: Birds--Flight--Juvenile fiction. | Birds--Nests--Juvenile fiction. | Determination (Personality trait)--Juvenile fiction. | Cooperation--Juvenile fiction. | CYAC: Birds--Flight--Fiction. | Birds--Nests--Fiction. | Determination (Personality trait)--Fiction.
Classification: LCC PZ7.1.D68 Be 2017 | DDC [E]--dc23

For more information or to contact the author, please go to
www.MichaelDotsikas.com.

Dedication

To my wife Dina for her encouragement and unwavering support and for helping me craft the story of Benjamin Birdie, and to my children for making me proud of the kind and gracious people they are.

Dream, Believe, Achieve!

—**Michael**

Dedicated to my mom for always believing in me, my dad for giving me all the tools I've ever needed to succeed, and to all the animal friends in my life for being my inspiration and reason for being.

—**Morgan**

Thank you to our Contributors:
Dina Dotsikas (editor)
Tony Testa (contributing editor)
Brittany Romanoff (dust jacket copy)

Special thanks to Lisa Rojany and
Ruth Beach for their invaluable feedback.

Benjamin Birdie gazed endlessly
high in a tree,
longing to be like the other birds
flying so free.

While anxiously waiting to take his first flight,
"I'm ready to fly!" he proclaimed with delight.

But **Mama Birdie** then warned to his utter dismay,
"You're **NOT** yet ready to fly, though you will be . . . **someday.**"

But **Benjamin Birdie** was *sure* he could fly.
And **NOW** was the time to give it a try.

He waited till Mama
went off to get lunch.
Then tried to find courage;
he needed a bunch.

Up, up and away...

he started to soar,
flapping faster and faster,
he pushed himself **more**.

"I'm flying! I'm flying!" he hollered with glee.
"I'm just like the other birds. **Look at M-E-E-E-E-E!**"

S u d d e n l y . . .

Benjamin Birdie's Smile
flipped to a Frown
as he was headed . . .
down . . . down . . .

D-O-O-O-O-O-W-N-N !

"Help me! I'm falling!" he desperately yelled, to all the tree dwellers he passed as he fell . . .

and fell . . .

and F-E-E-E-E-E-E-L-L-L-L!

Tumbling and bouncing,
bumpety-bump!

He crashed to the ground,
thumpety-thump!

Then he slowly looked up, filled with despair.
"How'll I ever get back . . . .
all the **w-a-a-a-y-y** there?"

He greeted an animal as **BIG** as can be,
"Please help me to my nest at the top of this tree."

"Of course! Without a doubt!" bragged the **TOWERING** beast.
"I'll take you there at once. No trouble in the least."

"Now climb aboard and hold on tight.
Sit back, relax, enjoy your flight."

The elephant flapped
his **HUGE** ears;
flying seemed like a cinch.
But off the ground
he didn't budge . . .
not even an INCH!

The elephant thought he could fly, yet was quite wrong,
and sadly just passed **Benjamin Birdie** along.

Staring at a creature S-O-O-O-O-O-O-O-O much TALLER than he,
Benjamin asked, "Please help me to my nest at the top of this tree."

"**Why certainly!**" the giraffe said, matter-of-factly.
"I'll stretch far as I can, and we'll reach it exactly."

"Jump on my head
and grab hold of my ear.
Ready . . . Set . . . Go !
Little bird, have no fear."

Stretching and **S-t-r-e-e-e-e-e-t-c-h-i-n-g** with **Benjamin** in tow.
Did she reach the treetop? Why certainly **NO!**

The giraffe thought
she could stretch far,
yet was quite wrong,
and sadly just passed
Benjamin Birdie along.

Surrounded by a serpent as
l-o-o-o-o-o-o-o-o-o-o-o-o-o-o-o-o-o-o-n-n-g
as can be,
Benjamin begged, "Please help me to my nest
at the top of this tree."

"Oh **sss**urely!" the snake said.
"But I in**ssss**iss**s**t we not climb.
I'll **sss**pin like a twi**sss**ter and
whi**sss**k you there in no time."

"Now **sss**lide on my back,
hold **sss**steady mo**sss**t of all.
I **sss**pin **sss**uper fa**sss**t
and wouldn't want you to fall."

Whirling and twirling
straight into a
fizzy.

They didn't get very far,
but sure did get
dizzy.

The snake thought he
could spin to the top,
yet was quite wrong,
and sadly just passed
Benjamin Birdie along.

With a bound from below sprang a tree kangaroo and said, "G'day, little fella. Why so blue?"

"It's not a good day." Benjamin replied, sad as can be. "No one can help me to my nest at the top of this tree."

"No worries mate," the 'roo said.
"I know the way.
Climb in, and I'll hop to the top
right away."

But . . .

. . . as it happened,
he didn't hop all that far,
suddenly startled by a
snoo-Z-z-z-ing jaguar.

The kind kinkajou tried hard but was just **too** small.

The cowering cuscus was **too** afraid to fall.

The sloth was **too** s-l-o-o-o-o-o-o-o-w, the porcupine **too** prickly.

The tarsier **too** timid, and ran away quickly.

The flying lemur, the flying squirrel;
both **"not meant"** to fly.
And unlike **Benjamin Birdie**,
they did not care to try.

The snooty tamarin was
way *too* proud.

The howler monkey,
way *too*
L-O-O-O-O-U-D!

The gibbons groomed
without making a peep.

"Shhhhh, don't wake
the night owls,"

who-o-o were sound asleep.

As **Benjamin Birdie** looked up
feeling hopeless and gray,
he suddenly noticed his nest
only inches away!

"H-O-O-O-R-A-A-Y!"

He skipped up the last branch
and flipped into his nest.
He was finally home.
Home is truly the **BEST!**

"I made it! I made it!"
he happily cheered.
"All because of my friends who
helped me get here."

Mama Birdie, returning later that day, asked, "Anything happen while I was away?"

Benjamin Birdie admitting without any delay,
"I'm **NOT** yet ready to fly, though I will be . . . *someday.*"

Meet the Tree Dwellers

Elephant
[**el**-*uh-fuh* nt]
(endangered species)

Elephants are the largest of all land animals, reaching heights of 13 feet and weights of over 16,000 pounds. Elephants prefer to live in areas with a mix of grasses, low woody plants, and trees. At midday, elephants rest under the trees, usually dozing off while standing. They spend up to 16 hours a day eating and can consume hundreds of pounds of food per day. Today, some elephant species are considered endangered due to the loss of habitat and illegal poaching.

Giraffes are the tallest of all land animals and can grow up to 20 feet tall. Their very long necks can grow to over 6 feet in length. Giraffes mostly eat leaves, fruits, flowers, and the twigs of trees, which provide an important source of calcium and protein to sustain their growth rate. Giraffes usually sleep less than 4 hours per day, taking quick power naps each lasting 2 to 6 minutes—sometimes even while standing!

Giraffe
[j*uh*-**raf**]
(threatened species)

Snake
[sneyk]
(some snake species are endangered)

Tree Kangaroo
[tree kang-g*uh*-**roo**]
(threatened species)

Tree kangaroos are solitary animals that spend almost their entire lives in the trees. They are very agile and can leap up to 30 feet from one tree to the next, as well as leaping 60 feet from the trees to the ground without getting hurt. These small mammals average between 16 and 30 inches long, with their tails usually longer than their bodies, reaching lengths of 34 inches.

Green tree snakes are an arboreal species and spend most of their time in the trees and shrubs. They secure themselves to their perch by wrapping their bodies and tails around the tree branches. When full grown, these reptiles can reach lengths of 5 feet, with some very large specimens growing to around 6.5 feet. When frightened, the green tree snake releases an unpleasant musky odor that wards off predators.

Jaguar
[jag-wahr]
(endangered species)

The jaguar is an elusive animal that spends most of its time either resting in the safety of the trees or hunting in the dense undergrowth. Jaguars have the strongest bite force of all cats. They are the third-largest feline species, weighing up to 200 pounds and reaching body lengths of over 6 feet long. A jaguar is a highly successful predator due to its strength, great hunting and hiding skills, and excellent climbing ability. In addition, unlike most cats, jaguars are very good swimmers.

Kinkajou
[king-kuh-joo]
(protected species)

Kinkajous are small rainforest mammals with body lengths of 16–24 inches. Nocturnal and arboreal, they spend most of their waking hours up in trees and sleep in the safety of tree hollows. Kinkajous have a special characteristic that helps them get termites from termite mounds, honey from hives, and nectar from flowers. It's their very long tongue, which can grow up to 5 inches long—almost a quarter of their body length!

Cuscus
[kuhs-kuhs]
(endangered species)

The cuscus is a small arboreal mammal averaging 18 inches in length and weighing around 12 pounds. It has thick woolly fur and a long, strong prehensile tail that aids in climbing. The cuscus spends its life almost exclusively in the trees, resting during the day and searching for food through the night. An elusive and very secretive animal, it is extremely difficult to find in the wild. It is said to be one of the most rewarding sights if you spot a cuscus in its natural habitat.

Sloth
[slawth]
(some sloth species are endangered)

Sloths are solitary, tree-dwelling mammals that pass their time sleeping and eating. Due to their lack of muscle tissue, sloths are the slowest moving land mammals, moving at speeds of around 6 feet per minute. They move so slowly that algae has enough time to grow on their long hair. The algae helps the sloths camouflage in the trees and is also used to feed their young. Sloths have long, sharp claws, which they use to get a good grip when climbing trees or hanging from branches and to defend against predators. A sloth's diet consists mostly of leaves, plants, and insects.

Porcupine
[**pawr**-ky*uh*-pahyn]
(some porcupine species are vulnerable)

The porcupine is the prickliest of all rodents and can be found inhabiting the forests and jungles of North America, South America, Asia, Europe, and parts of Africa. Porcupines are covered with as many as 30,000 sharp, needle-like quills ranging from 3 to 12 inches in length. These quills can be detached very easily and are used to defend against predators. Any animal that attacks a porcupine can easily end up with sharp quills in their skin. These quills are venomous and very difficult and painful to extract. Porcupines quickly grow new quills to replace the ones they lose.

Tarsier
[**tahr**-see-er, -see-ey]
(some tarsier species are endangered)

Tarsiers are tiny nocturnal and arboreal mammals growing to about 5 inches long and weighing around 5 ounces. They spend most of their lives clinging to vertical tree branches where they rest during the day. They are also known to have the largest eyes of any mammal in relation to their body size (each eye is actually heavier than its brain and larger than its stomach). Tarsiers have unusually long anklebones which enable them to jump distances more than 40 times their own body length. These bones are known as tarsals, which is where the tarsier gets its name.

Flying Lemur
[**lee**-mer]
(threatened species)

The flying lemur is an arboreal mammal that uses a thin, blanket-like membrane extending between its front and hind limbs to glide (*not fly*) through the jungle in silence. Some flying lemurs were measured gliding over 400 feet through the forest. Clumsy and awkward animals, flying lemurs move slowly and cling spread-eagled to tree trunks. They sleep in old tree holes and feed on leaves, flower buds, and tree sap. When resting, flying lemurs hang upside down while clutching branches with their strong claws.

Flying Squirrel
[**skwur**-*uh* l]
(some flying squirrel species are endangered)

Flying squirrels are small, highly social mammals (12 inches long and weighing 6 ounces) that have a furry, stretchy membrane that stretches between their front and back legs. When the flying squirrel needs to get away quickly, it opens its arms and legs out and uses the membrane like a parachute, gliding 30 or more feet from tree to tree. Flying squirrels also have large eyes and stubby, flattened tails. There are nearly 50 different species of flying squirrel found in forests around the world.

Tamarin
[tam-*uh*-rin, -ran]
(endangered species)

he golden lion tamarin is one of
he smallest primates in the world,
with the average adult growing to
ust 8 inches tall. It spends the
majority of its life inhabiting and
moving around in the trees. The
golden lion tamarin's sharp nails,
which are clawlike in appearance,
elp it to move around and climb
rees more easily. It also has a very
ong nonprehensile tail, which is
ften longer than its body.

Howler Monkey
[hou-ler muhng-kee]
(endangered species)

Howler monkeys are considered to be
the loudest land animal, able to project
their howling voices for up to 3 miles.
They use their loud voices to defend their
territory. Howler monkeys are one of the
largest species of monkey, growing to
4 feet tall. Despite their large size, they
weigh less than 22 pounds. This allows
them to move through the high trees with
more agility and lets them hang from
branches by their very long prehensile
tails when picking fruit.

Gibbon
[gib-*uh* n]
(endangered species)

ibbons are small-sized apes
rowing to 3 feet tall and weighing
round 15 pounds) that spend the
ajority of their lives in the trees. They
e very social and spend a lot of time
ooming each other. Gibbons have
ry long arms which are often longer
an their legs. They use their arms to
elp them to move around in the trees
d to balance while walking along
anches. Gibbons are the fastest
onflying tree-dwelling mammals in the
orld, moving at speeds of up to 35
ph and able to swing themselves 50
et from tree to tree. They are also
credible at leaping and can leap
ng distances of up to 26 feet.

Night Owl
[nahyt oul]
(some owl species are endangered)

Owls are believed to be among the
smartest of all birds. Owls are almost
always nocturnal, active only at night
and sleeping high in the trees during
the day. The female owls of almost all
the species are about 25 percent
larger than the males. Owls are able
to fly silently and have exceptional
vision and hearing, making them very
good hunters. Antarctica is the only
place in the world where there are no
species of owls found. The least
pygmy owl is the smallest owl in the
world at about 4 inches tall, and the
Eurasian eagle owl is the largest owl
in the world at about 28 inches tall.

Glossary:

arboreal - living in or among trees

camouflage - something (such as color or shape) that protects an animal from attack by making the animal difficult to see in the area around it

elusive - hard to find or capture

endangered species - a group of related animals that have become rare and are at risk of extinction because of human activity, changes in climate, or changes in their environment

feline - belonging to the cat family classification of animals

habitat - the place or type of place where an animal naturally lives

mammal - a type of animal that breathes air, is warm-blooded, has a backbone, grows hair on its body, and feeds milk to its young

nocturnal - active mainly during the night

poaching - to hunt or catch an animal illegally

predator - an animal that lives by capturing and eating other animals

prehensile - capable of grabbing or holding something by wrapping around it

primate - group of animals that includes humans, apes, and monkeys

protected species - a species of animal which it is forbidden by law to harm or destroy

reptile - a type of animal that is cold-blooded, lays eggs, and has an outer covering of horny scales or plates

solitary - living alone; without companions

species - a group of animals that are similar and have some shared quality

threatened species - a species that is likely, in the near future, to become an endangered species within all or much of its range

venomous - poisonous; harmful and unpleasant

vulnerable species - a group of related animals which is likely to become endangered unless the circumstances threatening its survival and reproduction improve; vulnerability is mainly caused by habitat loss or destruction of the species' home

About the Author

Author **Michael Dotsikas** is the creator of Benjamin Birdie—the little bird with a BIG dream! Michael lives in Manorville, New York, with his wife, Dina, their blended family of five amazing children, and two precious pups. Michael was born in Greece and immigrated to the United States with his family when he was four. In addition to his passion for creating stories for children, Michael is the owner of a computer consulting company he founded in 1995. Traveling and spending time with family and friends are favorite pastimes.

Visit Michael at **www.MichaelDotsikas.com.**

About the Illustrator

Morgan Spicer is an illustrator, a concept/character designer, animal advocate, ethical vegan, TV/film fanatic, and the proud parent of three rescue dogs. Morgan Spicer works in NYC and has illustrated fifteen books while also creating custom animal art for her Bark Point Studio followers and animal rescue partners. It is her ultimate goal to open her own animal rescue, sanctuary, and studio (Bark Pointé) to continue educating youth about the magic, friendship, and responsibility that comes with animal companionship and the importance of cherishing nature.

Check out her other works at **BarkPointStudio.com.**

Look for upcoming books in the Benjamin Birdie series.

All Aboard the Circus Train

BIG TOP EXPRESS

Written By
Michael Dotsikas

Illustrated By
Morgan Spicer

First in a series of fun, interactive, clever rhyming books with socially mindful themes.